On loan from the School Libraries Resources Service.
Please return by the end of the current term.
Telephone: 020 8359 3931   Fax: 020 8201 3018
Email: slrs@barnet.gov.uk

www.libraries.barnet.gov.uk

BARNET
LONDON BOROUGH

ReadZone Books Limited

First published in this edition 2015

© in this edition ReadZone Books Limited 2015
© in text Hilary Robinson 2004
© in illustrations Belinda Worsley 2004

Hilary Robinson has asserted her right under the Copyright Designs and Patents Act 1988 to be identified as the author of this work.

Belinda Worsley has asserted her right under the Copyright Designs and Patents Act 1988 to be identified as the illustrator of this work.

Every attempt has been made by the Publisher to secure appropriate permissions for material reproduced in this book. If there has been any oversight we will be happy to rectify the situation in future editions or reprints. Written submissions should be made to the Publisher.

British Library Cataloguing in Publication Data (CIP) is available for this title.

Printed in Malta by Melita Press.

ISBN 978 1 78322 136 3

Visit our website: www.readzonebooks.com

Batty Betty's Spells

by Hilary Robinson

illustrated by Belinda Worsley

Batty Betty always found

...she got her spells
mixed up.

So when she tried to mend a plate, it turned into a...

cup!

Her very worst day of all
was when she blocked
the sink.

She cast a spell to sort it out
and turned her black cat...

pink!

Things did not get better
when she started
a spring clean.

The spell for this
went very wrong and
turned her pink cat...

green!

Ah, she thought, I know a spell to make my messy bed.

But when she waved
her magic wand,
it turned her green cat...

red!

Betty mixed a magic spell to clean her bathroom pipes.

But oh dear me – her
poor red cat was...

head to foot in
stripes!

Betty then gave up
on spells,
and took her broom
and mac.

She flies around the sky at night...

28

29

... so her striped cat looks

black!

Did you enjoy this book?

Look out for more *Redstart* titles –
first rhyming stories for beginning readers